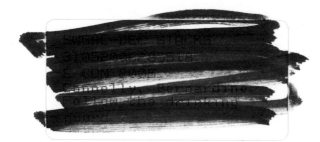

ABDO Publishing Company is the exclusive school and library distributor of Rabbit Ears Books.

Library bound edition 2005.

Library of Congress Cataloging-in-Publication Data

Connelly, Bernardine.
  Follow the drinking gourd / written by Bernardine Connelly ; illustrated by Yvonne Buchanan.
      p. cm.
  "Rabbit Ears books."
  Summary: A young slave girl sets off north with her brother and mother, following the star in the Drinking Gourd, or Big Dipper, that points to freedom.
  ISBN 1-59197-763-0
  1. Underground railroad—Juvenile fiction. [1. Underground railroad—Fiction. 2. Slavery—Fiction. 3. African Americans—Fiction.] I. Buchanan, Yvonne, ill. II. Title.

PZ7.C761859Fo 2004
976.8'04'092—dc22
[E]—dc22

                                                              2004046698

All Rabbit Ears books are reinforced library binding
and manufactured in the United States of America.

ABDO
Publishing Company

FOLLOW THE DRINKING GOURD

WRITTEN BY
BERNARDINE CONNELLY

ILLUSTRATED BY
YVONNE BUCHANAN

RABBIT EARS BOOKS

Twilight's just fallen, the day's cotton's been counted and carded, and out in the night, just past the willow tree, you hear the quail whistle out to you, *bob-bob-white, bob-bob-white*, and that song sprouts up at the back of your throat about following the Drinking Gourd, about Peg Leg Joe, about escaping North to freedom. But as much as you want to sing it, you don't say a word. You just think it. Follow the Drinking Gourd. It's time to run.

Mary Prentice was only eleven years old when her mama decided to escape. See, Mary, her mama, and her brother, Samuel, were slaves on the Darby cotton plantation in a little town just outside Mobile, Alabama. Their papa used to be there with them, except he'd been sold when Mary was only six years old. So, as it was, all three of them picked cotton—even Mary— six days a week. It was hard work, tiring work.

There was something special about Mary—she had a peculiar knack for gathering stories. She had ears sharp enough to pick up even the quietest whispers that might be floating about.

One evening, right after dinner, Mary snuck down to the stables. She probably should have been helping Mama with the evening chores, but that night she was extra curious because she'd heard mention about Mr. Darby sending some of the slaves to auction.

The stable was an awfully dark and drafty place to visit at night, and what with all the rows of stalls and the nooks and crannies for the feed and the tack, it seemed like an enormous

maze. When Mary got there the stables were quiet, but it didn't take long for her to overhear some stable hands whispering down at the far end of the stalls.

"Going to send five slaves. That's what I heard Mr. Darby saying. I even heard tell they'd be selling the Prentice boy as well."

Mary's face grew hot as an iron, but she stayed tight against the bin. Maybe she'd heard wrong. She wanted to run up and ask them, but they'd just shoo away a little girl like her. The voices grew softer, and then shut off immediately when someone started banging hard on the paddock gate. Why had the men stopped talking? Mary ran to see who would be making that kind of noise.

He was a wild-looking fellow, and he was hammering away fast and hard, but it didn't look like he was getting too much work done. Mary hung back a little to watch him. He was what they liked to call a journeyman because he traveled about doing carpentry and smithing. He had rough clothes, a mass of curly hair, and, on his right side, a peg leg. Mary's mind was swirling with the news about Samuel, but she couldn't help watching the man. Even above all the noise he was making, he kept singing the same little song:

"When the sun comes back, and the first quail cries,
Follow the Drinking Gourd.
For the old man is waiting for to carry you to freedom
If you follow the Drinking Gourd."

Mary was about to creep back to see if she could hear more from the stable hands, when she saw Mr. Darby coming down the path. Quickly and quietly she whisked herself away. Before she left, Mary took one last look at this peg-legged man, and maybe she was seeing funny, but it really looked as if he winked right in her direction.

Mary ran down the path to home, her feet shooting up dust and her mind heavy with the news about Samuel. Before she knew it, she was singing that song. She must have sung it a good twenty times when—*thwop!*—Mama clamped her hand right smack over Mary's mouth.

"Mary Prentice, where'd you go learning that song?"

Mama's eyes were staring at her brighter than Mary had ever seen them.

"Song, Mama? Why, I just sort of picked it up from that peg-legged journeyman working in the stables. Did Papa ever talk about a journeyman like that? He sure was odd. Over and over, he wouldn't sing nothing else."

That night Mama took Samuel and Mary out to the willow tree, out where nobody could hear, and she held them close as she told them about the song of the Drinking Gourd.

"Look up to where you see the Big Drinking Gourd there overhead."

Mama looked at the stars and pointed to what they sometimes called the Big Dipper and sometimes the Big Drinking Gourd, since it looked just like the big gourd they drank water out of when they worked in the fields.

Mama went on, "Now follow it to the Little Drinking Gourd just beyond it, and right there at the tip of the handle you can see that star shining bright like it's looking right toward you. That's the North Star."

Mary stared up at that North Star like she was trying to memorize it, while Mama explained that the peg-legged man was called Peg Leg Joe, and that he wasn't just a carpenter passing through town. He'd known Papa, and he was

an agent for the Underground Railroad. So maybe Peg Leg Joe's wink wasn't just her imagination—but did this mean that Mama was talking about escaping North? About *them* escaping North?

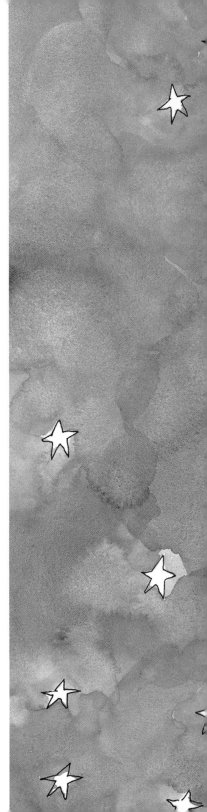

Mama's voice was hushed and serious:

"The old man is waiting—that's Peg Leg Joe himself; he'll be the one to help us cross the river into the North. *The first quail cries* means the best time to go is spring. The weather's right and the river's high. *Left foot, peg foot, traveling on*—we'll be following Peg Leg Joe's path. Peg leg on the right, footprint on the left."

The riverbank makes a very good road,
The dead trees will show you the way.
Left foot, peg foot, traveling on,
Follow the Drinking Gourd.

The river ends between two hills,
Follow the Drinking Gourd.
There's another river on the other side,
Follow the Drinking Gourd.

When the great big river meets the little river,
Follow the Drinking Gourd.
For the old man is waiting for to carry you to freedom,
Follow the Drinking Gourd.

Mary so wanted to ask the one question that kept biting at her—did this mean she might see her papa?

Next day, Mary's mother handed her something in a small red cloth and told her to run to the stables and give it to Peg Leg Joe. Mary didn't know what it was, but she knew it would be their signal to say they were ready to go. There he was, hammering away in the same place he had been before. At first he paid Mary no mind, and Mary wasn't sure that they could really trust him.

"The riverbank makes a very good road,
The dead trees will show you the way.
Left foot, peg foot, traveling on,
Follow the Drinking Gourd."

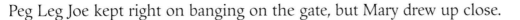

Peg Leg Joe kept right on banging on the gate, but Mary drew up close.

The hammering grew softer, so she asked him, "But how do we get to the river?"

"Your mama knows."

"My mama knows no such thing. She's never left the plantation," said Mary.

"Your mama doesn't say all she knows, but she's got a map of the route right in her head, only she's going to need your help. Now, your papa's told me about you. He said you were as brave as they come and that you had enough stories in that head of yours to fill a shelf of books."

Her papa! Had Peg Leg Joe seen him? Mary would've jumped up to ask all about it, only Peg Leg Joe's eyebrows tightened together and he began hammering harder than ever, and out of the corner of her eye, Mary could see that Mr. Darby was heading right down toward the stables. As she rushed to get to the back gate, she dropped the cloth and out of it fell a small wooden object, about the size of her thumb.

It was a tiny drinking gourd, and Mary knew by looking at it that Papa must have whittled it himself. There wasn't time to run back, so she tossed the little gourd straight to Peg Leg Joe and waited to watch him catch it. Before long she was back on the path to home, but she was sure she could hear Peg Leg Joe say, "I'll be seeing you at the river."

That night, Mama brought Mary and Samuel back out to the willow tree and wrapped them up in extra sets of clothes. Not a single word came across Mama's lips, but Mary knew that this was it; it was time to run. Mary took a good look at the North Star to make sure it was looking out for them, and off she went, one step behind Samuel and two steps behind Mama, who carried only a cotton sack of food and the great big walking stick Papa had carved for her.

They had to get to the Tombigbee River before dawn to hide their trail. When Master Darby found them missing, he was sure to set out with the hunting dogs. Mary's legs grew tired. It seemed like Mama and Samuel were running. Mary crouched down on a stone to rest, but Mama shook her awake. She gave her a biscuit from the sack and rubbed Mary's feet. They were sore and blistered.

When they made it to the river the sun was beginning to rise, and Mary could hear cocks crowing from a nearby farm. Mr. Darby would notice soon that they weren't in the fields. At the riverbank, Mama pointed to the ground with her walking stick. Left foot, peg foot—there were Peg Leg Joe's marks left for them to follow.

That day and for many days, they traveled the riverbank at night and hid during the day in nearby swamps and marshes. They followed Peg Leg Joe's footprints until, at one bend in the river, the prints disappeared. They still had the Drinking Gourd as their guide, but each day they grew more tired and hungry, and they ate less and less as the food began running out. That was when they decided that Samuel and Mary would hide out by the nearest plantation to see if they could get more food.

"If we are where I think we are, you'll find the slaves' quarters right next to the barn. Wait by the barn, and when it's pitch dark, you make the quail's call, nice and soft. And if you see a lantern light up in the slaves' quarters' four-paned window, there'll be someone to help you," said Mama.

Mary and Samuel waited until night to run. They hid by the barn and tried singing like the quail, *bob-bob-white, bob-bob-white*. No light came on. So they waited. And waited. When it was so dark they could barely see each other, sure enough, they saw a hand light a tiny lantern in the four-paned window. They leaned themselves hard against the barn, and before long, someone handed them a heavy cotton sack. Mary could see only the outline of a very old face and a man bent over with age.

"They've seen you, Mary and Samuel." The man's voice was a whisper.

"How d'you know our names?" asked Mary.

"There are posters up all over town. Your master's been sending out the alarm up the whole river."

"But where do we go if we can't use the river?" Samuel asked.

"There's pepper in the sack. Shake it after you if the dogs are near. It gets them off your trail. And follow the Drinking Gourd. If you make it past this stretch, you'll only have a few more days of following the river. And when you reach the Tennessee River, there are good people there—Quakers. They'll know you're coming. They helped your papa."

"How will they know?" She waited to hear more, but there was no answer. The old man was gone.

Mary, Samuel, and Mama took to the woods. The river was no longer safe. They moved slowly, fighting the vines and undergrowth. It didn't help to think that there were people after them ready to catch them for money. Mary and Samuel shook the pepper behind them, and as much as she had hated the murky water and squishy mud, Mary wished she were back by the river.

Mary was first to hear the dogs. Mama said to pay them no mind, that they might just be chasing rabbits, but as the barking came closer, the three knew they'd better do something. The river was too far to run back to, so Mama threw the rest of the pepper onto the ground and pulled Mary and Samuel into a cascade of hundreds of kudzu vines. There was a small hollow place just large enough for them to crouch into. The three of them squatted low and so close together it was hard to tell one heartbeat from another. Mama gripped them tight.

The dogs were getting close, barking louder, faster, as if they knew just where the three were. Before long there were horse hooves and brusque voices coaxing the dogs on.

"Thousand dollars for the boy. Come on, dogs, track 'em down!"

Mary waited, sure they were caught. She could hardly believe it when the dogs stopped barking and started to whine. The pepper had worked! She saw Mama's mouth loosen into a smile.

A few days later, Mary, Samuel, and Mama came upon a clearing in the woods, and beyond it, a small town. It surely wasn't a place the three of them could walk into. In fact, there were probably posters right there with descriptions of them. But there, on the other side of the town, was the Tennessee River.

That night, the three of them slipped through the clearing like cats. Then Mary heard something—footsteps—and they were close. The three darted over to a cemetery and hid behind the biggest tombstone they could reach. But the footsteps kept after them.

"Art thou not Esther Prentice?"

Mama didn't say a word, but Mary saw her lift up her head, slowly. It was a Quaker man. He had a neatly trimmed beard shaped just along his jawbone. The man explained that they were in great danger. There were slave catchers looking for them all about the two rivers, the Tennessee and the Ohio. He said that if they could make it to his boat, moored just at the dock, then he could take them safely straight up the Tennessee River. With Mama in the lead, they made themselves invisible, darting from building to building, crouching low and scarcely breathing.

When they reached the boat, Mary's eyes opened wide with wonder when she saw the secret compartment under the deck. She and her family slipped down into it and listened while the Quaker man and his wife and son piled sack upon sack of flour and dry goods over the secret door.

That next morning Mary and her family traveled up the Tennessee in broad daylight, without even a single slave catcher guessing where they might be.

The Quaker man warned them that their last stop, the Ohio River, was rife with patrols, and even Peg Leg Joe couldn't guard against that. As the song said, the river—the Tennessee—ends between two hills and there's another river on the other side.

It took days to find any trace of Peg Leg Joe. It was Mary who spotted the prints—left foot, peg foot—and they raced to the end of the path to find a tiny inlet tucked into the hills. There they found more prints, but Peg Leg Joe was nowhere to be seen.

Mary felt her heart drop, and her eyes grew hot with tears. But then, to her amazement, out from behind the trees stepped Papa. Papa! Mary thought it was a dream, but Papa gripped her hand tight and placed in it

the tiny drinking gourd! Papa looked tired, but he pulled Mama, Samuel, and Mary as close as he could and held on to them. Mary wasn't sure he would ever let go. He said that all along the way he'd heard about Mama and her two brave children, and that that had given him the courage to run almost without stopping. There was lots to tell, but they still were not across the river. At nightfall, Papa took them by the hand and led them forward to Peg Leg Joe. When they reached the cove where Peg Leg Joe's boat was hidden, he was waiting for them.

The moon hid behind the clouds to let them cross, and the river frogs seemed to be croaking especially hard to wish them luck. Peg Leg Joe rowed them across, soft and quiet as swans, right past the patrols until the boat slowed and, with a soft bump, they came to the other side of the river. They still had a journey ahead of them before they were entirely safe, but this was it. They were together and on their way to freedom, and Mary could hear herself telling the story of their escape over and over in the days to come.

The riverbank makes a very good road,
The dead trees will show you the way.
Left foot, peg foot, traveling on,
Follow the Drinking Gourd.

The river ends between two hills,
Follow the Drinking Gourd.
There's another river on the other side,
Follow the Drinking Gourd.

When the great big river meets the little river,
Follow the Drinking Gourd.
For the old man is waiting for to carry you to freedom,
Follow the Drinking Gourd.